Broken &

Abused

The Imprisoned Mind

Broken & Abused
The Imprisoned Mind

Broken &
Abused
The Imprisoned Mind

Broken & Abused
The Imprisoned Mind

Broken &

Abused

The Imprisoned Mind

Broken & Abused
The Imprisoned Mind

Table of Contents

Table of Contents

Table of Contents

Table of Contents

Foreword

Love.
We all want love.
We all yearn for the affection that comes with
being in love.
We all desire the attention that comes with being in
a relationship.
We all envision having someone to call "forever"
and someone to rely on for unconditional support.
We experience falling in love as a feeling of
euphoria, an experience that leaves us breathless
and on edge.
However, with love, comes intrapsychic battles.
Perpetual war with our own minds.

Fighting to desperately maintain a grasp on a
transient emotion.
Struggling to accept failure even when we have
been defeated.
Holding onto lust even when love ceases and when
infatuation destroys us.
Falsely believing that deceit and manipulation
represent strength and willpower.
Displaying carefully constructed masks over true
personalities.
Crying out for help in silence.
Unnoticed.
Unseen.
Hidden.
Gone.

Prologue

She is a young girl.
Kind-hearted.
Thoughtful.
Compassionate.
Honest and Outspoken.
Always offering a helping hand.
Always sacrificing herself for others.
Never asking for favors in return.
Her life revolves around the demands and pleasures
of others.
She is respected.
Admired.

She climbs to the top of the success ladder in her
personal life journey.
She is confident.
She shines self-love.
She accepts herself and others, and she seeks to find
someone who accepts her in return.
She wants love.
All she ever wants in life is love.
She has all the qualities to be the perfect girlfriend.
She has all the qualities any man would want.
Why is she still alone?
Why is she still dreaming about a partner rather
than being with one?
Why is she still alone?
Will anyone love her?
Can anyone love her?
What is wrong with her?
Is she less attractive than she thinks?
Is she less intelligent than she believes?
Is she so severely flawed that everyone who
encounters her eventually flees?
Is she meant to be alone forever?
She believes she will never find someone.
She believes she will never find love.

She believes that if she does not change, she will die
alone.
She believes that she is unlovable.
She must take action.
Remove the face everyone is repulsed by and
replace it with a more attractive one.
Hide the personality that scares men away and
replace it with one that lures them in.
She must change.
Change every part of who she is if she ever wants to
be loved.
Change.
Change.
CHANGE.

Trapped

Drip.

Drip.

Drip.

The liquid from her face fastidiously drips, drop by drop, onto a puddle in front of her.

Blink.

Blink.

Blink.

She opens and closes her eyes as she stares toward the damp, cold ground beneath her.

Darkness consumes her.

She sniffles.

A single tear flows down the bridge of her perfectly constructed nose and drips off the tip.

Drip.

She blinks again.

Blink.

Blink.

Blink.

'Where am I?' she wonders.

Silence.

Still.

The air around her is quiet.

Her breath feels soft as she slowly inhales and exhales.

"Where am I?" she whispers softly.

Silence.

"Hello!? Is anybody there?" she shouts out into her surroundings.

Silence.

No response.

Still.

She sits in complete darkness, where she cannot even see her own two hands. She is not sure whether she should be scared or confused, whether she should be sad or angry.

She blinks again.

Blink.

Blink.

Blink.

This time, her eyes feel dry, but her face feels damp.

"What the hell?" she whispers, softly again, to herself.

She runs the fingers of her right hand across her eyes.

Nothing.

No tears.

Dry.

She runs the fingers of her right hand across her left cheek.

It feels wet.

Not thin like water, however, but dense and thick.

'What the hell can this be?' she wonders, confused, yet not afraid.

She brings the index finger of her right hand up to her nostrils and takes a whiff, hoping she can distinguish the mysterious substance on her face by its scent. It smells unusual. Familiar, but strange. For the life of her, she cannot identify this aroma.

She brings the same finger toward her mouth, her lips chapped and scabbed. Anxious, she sticks out the tip of her tongue and cautiously licks her finger.

Blood.

She tastes blood.

She has blood on her finger.

She has blood dripping down her face.

"Did I cut myself?" she asks herself, shuddering.

She does not feel pain. She does not feel injured. Yet, blood continues to run down her face, drop by drop.

Drip.

Drip.

Drip.

She feels around this time with the fingers from both hands for cuts, bruises, or scars on her face.

Nothing.

'Where the hell is this blood coming from?' she wonders.

Now she feels petrified.

Her face is mysteriously bleeding, and she is sitting in complete darkness with no one else around.

"I have to get out of here!" she whispers heavily to herself, trembling and shaking.

She attempts to stand up, only to smash her head against a hard surface above her, pushing her back onto the damp, cold ground.

"FUCK!" she cries out.

She attempts to crawl forward, only to strike her skull against another hard surface.

"SON OF A BITCH!" she cries out again.

To avoid the misfortune of colliding her head into another hard surface, she reaches both arms out and feels the environment around her. She is surrounded by nothing but the same hard surface on all sides. Like some sort of room.

"What the FUCK is going on?!" she screams.

She moves her hands around, feeling for a possible doorknob or a handle she can hopefully grasp onto and escape.

"There has to be a door. It's a room. All rooms have to have doors," she repeatedly whispers quietly to herself.

Nothing.

Not one bump.

Not one hole.

Gathering all her strength, she pushes her weight against one side, hoping she can force her way out.

The surface does not move.

She tries again on a different side. Again, the surface does not budge. She attempts to force her body weight against the remaining sides, hoping she can find a secret passageway. However, nothing seems to be shifting or moving.

"What the FUCK!?" she screams out.

She is starting to become angry and frustrated.

Then she realizes.

She is not trapped inside a room. She is trapped inside a box, a dark and compact box with nothing else around and no way out.

"LET ME OUT OF HERE!" she screams again as her throat begins to form a rash.

Silence.

No response.

No answer.

No one.

"GET ME THE FUCK OUT OF THIS SHITHOLE!" she screams with every power and strength she has remaining.

Silence.

No response.

No answer.

No one.

Taking both her fists, she begins pounding against the hard surfaces, thinking she can punch a hole through and see outside.

Thump.

Thump.

Thump.

The surfaces remain intact.

Then she hears an echo.

"Wait, what is that?" she asks herself.

She pounds again.

Echo.

She taps the surface lightly with the knuckles of her right hand.

Echo again.

"Metal?" she whispers to herself. "Am I surrounded by metal? Fuck, that's why no one can hear me. I'm surrounded by fucking metal in a fucking metal box for NO FUCKING REASON!" she freaks out as she becomes desperate.

"HELP ME!!!!" she screams and pounds her fists against the metal surfaces until her throat begins to pierce and her fists begin to bruise.

Silence.

Quiet.

Still.

"I KNOW YOU CAN HEAR ME!!!" she yells out. "Let me the FUCK OUT!"

Silence.

Quiet.

Still.

Except for the echo of her own screeching voice.

Whatever person or thing that locked her inside this metal box refuses to acknowledge her presence.

She remains silent, expecting to hear breaths or footsteps if she is, something to confirm that she is not alone.

Silence.

Quiet.

Still.

Nothing.

There is no one there. There is no one around.

All she can hear is her own breath and heartbeat.

All she can hear is her blood dripping onto the metal ground.

Desperate, she begins to claw the fingers of both her hands against the metal surface in front of her, as her fingernails screech in agony upon contact. Her ears pierce with pain, and her face cringes with the noise, but she does not care.

She continues scratching.

Scraping and scratching until her fingers begin to bleed. She winces in unbearable pain but continues to scratch. Her fingernails crack and break while the skin on her fingers tears and sheds. Blood pours profusely down her fingers and arms, but she continues. She refuses to quit until she sees an opening. She scrapes, and she scrapes until the noise changes. The once-screeching noise suddenly turns blunt.

"What the fuck?" she mutters to herself.

Nervous and anxious, she slowly brings her right hand toward her left hand and rubs her fingers together. She feels bone. The bones of her left-hand fingers rub against the bones of her right-hand fingers, crackling with each touch. She had been scraping so aggressively that she had filed through the skin of her fingers and down to her bones.

Tears now begin to heavily pour from her sunken eyes and down her jaunted cheeks. She cannot remember the last time she has eaten nor the last place she had been before this death-trap. Her memories seem to have completely faded, and all she can recall about her life is this moment, trapped inside this metal box.

She cannot remember having felt this much pain. Her fingers have shortened in length, and all she can feel are stumps in place of them. She feels nauseous from the intense suffocation and loss of blood and oxygen. However, with every strength she has remaining, she continues to scratch.

Bone against metal. Skin against bone. Blood against tears. She continues to abrasively grind her exposed bones against the rusty metal, screaming in anguish and affliction as all she hears is bone against metal. She closes her eyes and tries to push past the throbbing torment. The more she suffers, the quicker and more aggressively she scrapes against the metal surface.

Scrape.

Scrape.

Scrape.

Her eyes burn from excessive crying as shards of bone and skin fly toward her cornea. She screams out with every breath and continues to grind her bones against the metal walls until she finally collapses in a pool of her blood.

Lying in her blood, she feels her right arm pulsating beneath her as if needles are piercing through her skin, in one side and out the other. She can feel the remaining blood inside her body seep out through her missing limbs, as the blood then travels toward her scarred ankles.

"This is it," she whispers to herself, lying helplessly on the ground. "This is how I die."

With one last drop of tear from her right eye, dissipating in her blood as it drips onto the pool, she slowly closes her eyes and her breath softens.

Broken

Thrown across the living room, shattering her $400 glass coffee table as she lands on top of the broken shards of glass, she spits out blood and a loose tooth through her bleeding lips.

"I'm sorry! I'm sorry! I'm sorry for saying I don't trust you. I do trust you! I love you!" she cries out as she begs for mercy, holding her right hand out toward him, signaling him to stop.

She continues to repeat herself, tears streaming down her eyes, as her fiancé angrily storms toward her.

"I DON'T CARE! I DON'T CARE WHAT YOU HAVE TO SAY ANYMORE! I FUCKING HATE

YOU!" her fiancé shouts, loud enough for their neighbors to hear, as he continues to approach her.

He raises his right arm and abruptly slaps her across her face, bruising her left eye and cheek.

However, he does not stop there. Before she has the chance to wipe off the blood dripping from her nose and re-open her eye from the blunt trauma, he grabs her by her tangled brunette locks, twists them around his thick, pale fingers to ensure a tight grip, and violently slams her bruised forehead against the concrete brick wall.

"I WISH I NEVER MET YOU! I HATE YOU! I HATE YOU! THIS IS WHY I CHEAT ON YOU! YOU'RE A PIECE OF SHIT! YOU'RE NOTHING!" he screams as he continues to bash her head against the wall simultaneously, only stopping when he receives a text notification on his phone.

He abruptly drops her, taking a lock of her hair with him, and runs over to grab his phone, refusing to look back while she collapses onto the bloody carpet.

Surrounded by immense pain, she crawls across her living room, lacerating her knees on the shards of glass from the broken coffee table and leaving a trail of blood behind her as she moves.

Piercing her skin more and more with every step she takes, she eventually makes her way to her "safe-corner," also known as, "the one spot in the entire apartment she is solely paying rent for that she is allowed to call her own."

"I'm so sorry…," she whispers to him again as she continues crawling, her voice choking on the blood running down her throat.

She finally reaches her "safe-corner," turns toward the wall, and hugs her knees close to her chest. She cannot clean the blood from her face because any movement when he is in rage is forbidden and will cause more harm to her than she had just endured.

She wipes the fresh blood with the sleeves of her polyester sweater, the ugly and expensive polyester sweater he had forced her to buy for herself last month.

She tells herself that this will all be okay, that this is just another one of their chaotic episodes, and that he will eventually calm down and their relationship will go back to the way it was before: happily in love.

She continues to rock back and forth in her corner, gathering the strength to pull herself together so she can continue to keep their relationship alive.

Back and forth.

Back and forth.

Back and forth.

She tries to convince herself that he is still the passionate and altruistic man she had fallen in love with the first day she laid eyes on him seven years ago. She glances over at him while he lazily lounges in front of his computer, for the tenth consecutive week, scrolling through the naked pictures of his ex-girlfriends he had saved onto his hard drive and non-discretely pleasuring himself.

"Turn around, bitch! This is NONE of your BUSINESS!!" he yells without turning his head, as he catches her looking at him out of the corner of his left eye.

She slowly turns back around, facing the wall once again. She notices their initials on the wall, carved in with a pocket knife when they first moved into the apartment, promising to love each other forever.

She remembers that day clearly. They had just signed their 24-month lease and moved their red-velvet sofa into their empty 700+ square feet apartment on the first floor in the suburbs.

They were both exhausted from staying up the night before, watching movies on her laptop under the covers. They collapsed onto the sofa after placing it awkwardly in the middle of the living room and began tickling and kissing each other until they both rolled off onto the floor, breathless from nonstop laughter.

Rather than proceeding with moving in the rest of the furniture and their belongings, they had decided to both carve their initials into one corner of the apartment to commemorate their new life together as an engaged couple.

'What went wrong?' she thinks to herself as her mind flashes back to the present when a drop of blood from her forehead drips into her left eye.

Her mind questions to herself all the wrong choices she had made and all the events that had started off so right that have gone so wrong. She questions what she had done to cause her fiancé to go from loving her to loathing her. She questions what she could have done differently to prevent her relationship from becoming her personal nightmare.

She questions why he continues to stay with her when his hate toward her is so strong that he needs to turn to twenty other women in place of her. She questions why she is still in love with him even when he is beating her to near-death every single night.

She questions why she cannot develop the fortitude and strength to walk away permanently. She questions her self-worth and whether she had done something to deserve all this. She questions who she has become and whether she still deserves to live.

She closes her eyes, leans her head, still dripping with blood, against the dried blood stains on her off-white living room wall from previous beatings, defeated, and accepts that this is her life until the day she dies. With one last single tear falling from the corner of her right eye, she falls asleep.

Seduced

She leisurely walks inside the dim, frigid restaurant, shivering while surrounded by candlelit chandeliers and taxidermy décor. She approaches the front desk and notifies the host that she is meeting a blind date, as the host leads her around the sharp, crimson corner of the restaurant and points toward a tall man with clean-cut hair sitting on a cushioned chair.

She stands frozen for a few minutes, as she stares at the back of her supposedly blind date, his muscular shoulders and broad back turned toward her.

"That has to be him, right?" she whispers to herself.

However, she is still unsure. She is timid, and she has walked into situations before where she had met the wrong people claiming to be her dates, and she had been sexually and physically abused as a result of it.

Her last "blind date" turned out to be a stranger who had falsely represented himself as her date when her actual date ghosted her, bought her drinks, sexually assaulted her in the back of his run-down SUV, stole her phone and wallet, and pushed her out onto the curb in a dark alleyway in the middle of the night.

She begins having flashbacks of that traumatic night, the night that, still to this day, makes her face sweat and her heart pound whenever she encounters someone new. She almost wants to turn around and go home for the fear of the same situation happening.

But then she thinks back to the past few weeks where she had the most amazing connection with this man, this man who is perfect in every single way. She does not want to let go of the opportunity of finally meeting her soulmate just because of a slight chance that this man might not be who she thinks he is.

She fumbles through her purse for her phone and finds his name at the top of her text messages. He is the only person she has texted, day and night, for the past three weeks. She has been so enamored by him that she has disregarded everyone else and has devoted all her time and energy to him and him alone.

She reads the last conversation they had a short four hours ago, where she told him how nervous she is about meeting him in person because she fears that he will not like her or that he will ghost her like all the others have. She smiles when she reads his response.

How can I possibly not like you? You're the most beautiful and amazing woman I have ever met, and I've only known you for three weeks. I know we'll hit it off, and I promise you that we will have an amazing night. I can't wait to see you and have many, many more dates with you. More importantly, I can't wait to spend my life with you. With you, I feel whole, like I have finally found my soulmate. You get me. We connect, and I will never do anything to make you lose your trust in me. You make me so happy!

Still cautious and doubtful, she sends him a text saying, *Walking in now! Can't wait to meet you!* as she anxiously waits for his response.

She sees him take his phone out of his pocket and begin typing.

Seconds later, she receives a text back saying, *Awesome! See you soon, darling!*

She is now certain that this man is her date, the man she has been flirting with nonstop since he first messaged her on a popular dating app, saying, *We don't know each yet, but I have a strong instinct that we'll get along,* and the man she cannot stop thinking about every night as she falls asleep.

Quietly and nervously, she walks up behind him, taps him lightly on his left shoulder, and smiles.

As he turns around, she greets him, "Hey!! You made it! I'm so glad we finally get to meet in person! You look EXACTLY like your picture!"

She chuckles awkwardly, reaches out, and embraces him, her long arms wrap tightly around his muscular shoulders, as she instantly melts in his thick and brawny arms when he hugs her back.

"Haha!" he laughs robustly. "It's such a relief to hear that I look like me! I was starting to get worried that my face was replaced with someone else's, or worse, SOMETHING ELSE! I'm so happy I get to meet you too, darling. I've been waiting for this moment ever since the day we started talking so I can do this."

He speaks sensually as he leans his face down toward hers and kisses her passionately, his lips gliding up and down her lips, and his tongue twisting around her tongue, making her fall for him even more. They do not stop.

They both believe that this is "love at first sight," as their bodies send sparks flying each time their lips touch.

They continue to kiss sensually in the restaurant as if no one else is around, gazing lustfully into each other's eyes and refusing to let go of one another. She feels her heart sink. She feels her stomach skip. She truly believes that, after all this time, she has finally found the love of her life.

"Let's get out of here," he whispers into her right ear as he gently nibbles on her earlobe.

"What about dinner?" she asks as her stomach growls.

She has not eaten all day so she could look sexy and slim in her new $100 bodycon dress.

"I have a much better idea," he whispers again as he slithers his lips up and down the side of her neck, sending shivers down her spine.

He then leads her out of the restaurant and into his car.

Completely blinded by his enchantment, she does not question him or herself as she climbs into the passenger seat of his untidy Sedan. He drives them both to the nearest hotel, checks them into a room, and continues to kiss her erotically with his soft lips as they ride up the elevator to their room, sliding his hands under her dress and up along her inner thighs while gliding his tongue down her cleavage and kissing the top of her breasts.

She can feel his penis becoming erect as he gently brushes it back and forth against the outside of her lavender lace thong. She can feel herself becoming aroused. She begins to feel lustful and stimulated as she pulls one strap of her dress off her shoulder and fully exposes one of her breasts. He proceeds to circle her right nipple with his tongue and sucks it, arousing himself even more.

They finally reach their floor. Disheveled and partly undressed, she jumps onto him, still lustfully making out with him, as he carries her into their room and throws her onto the bed.

Out of the corner of her eye, as he continues to kiss her body, she notices that their room is unkempt. Dirty ashtrays and used tissues are left on top of the dressers. Curtains are partly detached, and the paint on the walls are chipped. Trashcans overflow with used condoms and toilet paper, and there is a stain on the bed next to her that appears to be urine.

However, despite her obsessive need for cleanliness, she does not care. All she wants is to make love to the man in front of her. She can see in his eyes that he wants her just as badly as she wants him.

She throws her logic out the door as she lies on the bed with his lips traveling down the brace of her neck and collarbones. She throws her common sense out the window as his hands slowly pull down her dress and caress her plump breasts and erect nipples.

His lips continue to travel. This time, down the rest of her body. He starts at her chest, breathing lightly on her breasts and circling her nipples with his tongue, makes his way down to her stomach, gently kissing her belly button as he continues down to her hips and upper thighs.

He removes her lace thong with his lips and teeth, licking and breathing on her waist as he does so. He pulls her thong down to her ankles, slides it over her neatly painted toenails, and removes it. He runs his hands and lips back up her legs, stroking and kissing her cleanly-shaved legs along the way.

He eventually reaches her vagina, the vagina he had been thirsty for since he first laid eyes on her profile picture, spreads her legs, and playfully teases her by running his fingers along her vaginal lips and softly rubbing her clitoris with his index finger.

She can feel herself pulsating as he inserts two fingers inside her and plays with her G-spot until she feels the pleasurable sensation overwhelm her.

He hungrily rubs his tongue on her engorged clitoris. She moans, feeling more pleasure than she has ever felt with any other man she had been with. She loves this man, this man she had only met two hours ago. But she does not care. She craves the feeling of his penis inside of her as her vagina begins to drip from the intense oral pleasure.

He rubs and licks her clitoris until she reaches orgasm, and she moans loudly enough for the entire floor to hear. He then makes his way back up to her face, kissing her naked body tenderly as he moves, eventually reaching her lips, and gives her a long and passionate kiss, thrusting his tongue down her throat.

"I want to taste you," she whispers into his ear as he gyrates his erect penis back and forth across her clitoris.

"I'm all yours," he whispers back as he becomes so overwhelmed with pleasure that he looks as if he is about to explode.

Stealing one more kiss, she proceeds to make her way down his body, undressing him one clothing item at a time. She eventually reaches his pants, carefully unbuckles his leather belt, and disrobes him. She can see his erection through his thin boxers.

Excited and ravenous for his penis, she pulls his boxers down, exposing his delicious and circumcised penis, the penis that she cannot wait to claim as hers.

She tosses his boxers onto the hardwood floor of the room and begins to stroke his penis with her hands. She licks her lips as she stares up at him, getting him more aroused. She then takes her tongue and licks him from the bottom of his shaft up to the tip of his penis, sending shivers through his body.

She repeats this several more times as she feels him getting more erect.

She opens her mouth and engulfs the tip of his penis, sliding her lips down as far as she can toward his testicles, and repeats this while stroking his scrotum as he nears orgasm.

"I want you, darling. I want to be inside of you," he moans vociferously as he can no longer control himself.

He sits up, flips her onto her back and slurps her vagina one more time.

"I love the way you taste. I wish I could eat you every day," he whispers to her as he floats his naked body on top of hers and inserts his thick and erect penis inside of her.

"You're so fucking wet," he moans as he passionately moves in and out of her.

He breathes onto her neck as he continues to thrust his penis in and out of her wet, tight vagina. She can feel him throbbing inside of her with every move. Within minutes, she reaches orgasm once again as he continues to make love to her.

In and out.

In and out.

In and out.

Until he reaches orgasm minutes later and ejaculates inside of her without a condom on. She can feel the warmth of his semen pour out inside of her. She does not care that they did not use a condom. She does not care about whether she will get pregnant. She does not care about whether she will get an STD. She does not care that she has not asked him if he is clean. She does not care that she just had sex with someone she barely knows, someone who was a stranger to her just yesterday.

All she cares about is him.

Them.

Their connection.

Their passionate love.

***

The first few weeks with her new boyfriend felt amazing. He is passionate and compassionate. He is empathetic and authentic. He sees a future with her, and he spends all his free time with her, talking about and planning their lives together. Just her.

He tells her that she is the most important and special woman in his world as he pictures his future family with her as his wife. He is the perfect boyfriend.

He says "good morning, darling" and "good night, love" to her every morning and every night, respectively, and he makes her feel like she is the only woman he ever wants for as long as he lives.

He trusts her enough to reveal his most private secret to her: that he is autistic. However, he reassures her that he is still functional and "normal." She does not care. She tells him that she accepts every part of him because she loves him and because she knows that he accepts every part of her.

"Everyone's a little different," she tells herself. "So, what if he's autistic? I have problems of my own too."

He tells her that he has never met anyone as endearing and as remarkable as her, and she continues to melt in his arms every time he smiles at her with his perfect lips and white teeth. He takes her out to all the best restaurants, goes with her to all her favorite concerts, and smiles at her charm when she dances or sings in public, never ashamed, never embarrassed.

He tells his family and friends that he cannot wait to spend the rest of his life with her and that she is the woman he is going to marry.

However, what really lures her in is his unconditional acceptance of her flaws and her scars. She tells him about her past traumas within their first week of dating, and he still accepts and loves her despite them. With open arms, he welcomes all her secrets. All the secrets she had been hiding from others for years.

He does not care that she has had a history of depression and suicidal behaviors. He does not care that she had been in and out of hospitals for her eating disorders. He does not care that she has had a history of sexual promiscuity, her deepest and darkest secret which she fears will drive love away from her forever.

He does not judge her. He does not criticize her. He does not care who she was or where she has been. He loves her. That is all he cares about.

Warned

About six months into the relationship, the dynamic between them begins to change. The man she had fallen in love with on their first date, the passionate and kind-hearted man who made her quiver with every touch, the non-judgmental and caring man who accepted every single flaw she possessed, suddenly becomes more critical about her appearance and the way she dresses.

She goes over to his apartment, which to get to requires two buses and one train ride with a travel time of four hours, one weekend, and as soon as she arrives, he throws open his apartment door and demands that she throw away every single item of clothing in her closet and purchase new ones, outfits which he would pick out for her, outfits which she would have to buy with her own hard-earned money, and that she begins wearing makeup that resembles that of an Egyptian goddess.

When she refuses to buy a certain sweater or a particular skirt because it is too expensive, or when she tries to reason with him to compromise on something she also likes, he throws tantrums inside the stores, behaving like a 4-year-old child and refusing to stop until she gives into his demands.

Five weeks and $2,200 later, she looks inside her closet. From ugly cotton sweaters to disgusting parachute pants and everything else in between, 90% of which still has tags on them, she questions whether the man she fell in love with actually fell in love with her as well, or whether he only fell in love with the idea of who she could be, with full intentions of changing every part of her.

But still, she loves him, so she lets it go, and she continues to adorn herself with the hideous garments he had chosen for her, losing herself behind layers of powder and ink just so he can maintain his pride and confidence.

Soon after, he asks her to move in with him as his best friend/roommate prepares to move out. Despite having to travel a longer distance to see her family and to go to her job, she reluctantly agrees, against her better judgment, because she knows it will make him happy.

He drives her to her parents' home, where she currently lives, to collect her belongings. Her mother, surprised from hearing for the first time that she is moving out, begs and begs her not to go. Her mother cries out and does everything she can to prevent her from walking out the door, including pulling her arm back and attempting to tie her down to a chair.

She starts arguments and physical fights with her mother as she hastily packs her belongings and grabs her 1-year-old canine. She keeps ignoring her mother's warnings that he is not good for her and that she is making a huge mistake by moving in with some boy she barely knows.

Deep down, she knows her mother is right. She knows that she is making a mistake, and she knows that she is not ready to live with someone she has only known for six months, but her infatuation continues to overpower her logic.

She violently pushes her mother onto the ground, shoves the rest of her clothing and toiletries into a plastic garbage bag, and bolts out into his car, without saying another word to her mother and without looking back, refusing to return her call for the next six months.

***

The first couple of weeks living in her new home with her new lover is everything she imagined it would be. He drives her to and picks her up from work. He takes her shopping and lets her pick out her birthday present, anything within a $10 budget. He cooks for her every morning and every night, and they make love every evening, caressing and holding each other until they fall asleep in each other's arms.

However, a month after she moved in, his demeanor begins to change again. He begins demanding for her share of the rent, telling her it is $700 a month, even though he promised her that she would not have to pay a single dime when she agreed to move in.

She tries to dispute him, saying that it is not rational for her to pay hundreds of dollars a month for a place she did not even choose and is barely living in since she works most of the time. But he ignores her. He insists that her salary of $30,000 a year is more than enough for her to spare $700 a month, and she is technically living there so she still has to pay.

He debates that she is being selfish by refusing to help him out when she knows that he makes substantially less than her. He guilt-trips her into shelling out an unnecessary $700 by saying that if she truly loves him, she would not have even hesitated to hand over the money.

Seven months after she begins paying her "half" of the rent, she notices that the more money she is handing over to him, the more time he is taking off from his own job, buying more video games and lavish gifts for himself such a brand-new computer chair and three new watches, and ordering delivery every night instead of cooking.

Suspicious, she pulls up the apartment listing on her laptop, searches for the price range of one-bedroom apartments and, to her surprise, finds out that the ENTIRE rent is only $700, not the $1,400 he had falsely led her to believe. She speaks up, livid and exasperated that she had been lied to.

"Hey, babe! What the hell is this?" she interrogates him as she continues to stare at the listing on her laptop screen.

"What the hell is what, honey?" he questions, with his eyes glued onto his computer monitor, oblivious to what she is asking.

"Have you been lying to me about the fucking rent?!" she demands as her tone begins to sharpen.

With his eyes still focused on his monitor and his right index finger monotonously clicking, he feigns ignorance to her words.

"I don't know what you're talking about, honey. I haven't lied to you about anything."

She storms over to him, laptop in hand with the apartment listing open, and shoves it in his face.

"It says RIGHT HERE that the ENTIRE rent is only $700, not $1,400 like you fucking told me it is."

He chortles.

"Oh, that? Yeah, they recently updated the prices because more people are moving in. It was double that when I rented it."

"You're lying," she says in disbelief. "You're a fucking liar."

"What the fuck are you talking about!? Stop fucking accusing me of shit!" he retorts as he becomes aggravated from the disturbance.

"You're fucking lying to me! It says here that the rent has been $700 a month for a one-bedroom apartment for the PAST 15 YEARS."

As she speaks, she suspects that her confrontation will not end well.

She knows, given his stubbornness, that he will somehow turn her words against her and make her the enemy. Even so, she continues to push him, with hopes that he will apologize to her and repay her what he owes her.

However, to her demise, he continues to act oblivious.

"What was that again? Sorry, I didn't hear you."

"IT SAYS HERE THAT THE RENT HAS BEEN $700 FOR THE PAST FIFTEEN FUCKING YEARS, YOU FUCKING LUNATIC!" she shouts at him as her patience begins to fade.

Her screaming grabs his attention. He turns to her, eyes finally peeled away from the screen.

"HEY! STOP FUCKING SCREAMING AT ME, YOU CUNT! I DIDN'T DO ANYTHING WRONG!"

"Do you want to explain this then?" her face turns red as she continues to hassle him for answers. "Have I been paying the entire FUCKING rent while you've been blowing money on stupid video games and dumb gifts!?"

Drained from hearing her scratchy voice complain while he is trying to play his game, he finally gives in.

"FINE! You've been paying the entire rent! So what?! I've been blowing money on you since the day we met!"

"Oh, you mean the whole $80 that you've spent on me compared to the $5,000 I've spent on this shitty land-fill apartment that I BARELY LIVE IN!?!"

Her voice begins to escalate. She can feel in her stomach that the next word that comes out of her mouth, aside from an apology, will only add fuel to the fire.

She questions to herself whether she should just back down now and apologize, whether she should just continue to hand over her salary without questions to avoid potentially ruining their relationship.

She opens her mouth, ready to apologize, when he interjects her with what proceeds to set her off.

"That's not the fucking point!" he asserts. "The point is, you make twice as much as I do. You should be paying the rent because you can afford it. I can't!"

Infuriated, she lashes back at him, regardless of what happens as a result.

"You can't fucking afford the rent because you DON'T EVEN GO TO WORK!! ALL YOU DO IS SIT ON YOUR LAZY ASS AND PLAY VIDEO GAMES WITH YOUR LOSER FRIENDS!! WE'RE SUPPOSED TO BE IN A PARTNERSHIP, BUT I'VE JUST BEEN TAKING CARE OF A LAZY FUCKING CHILD!!!"

"What I do with my own time is NONE OF YOUR BUSINESS!! I GO TO WORK WHEN I NEED TO, AND I DON'T FUCKING NEED YOU TO TAKE CARE OF ME! I NEVER ASKED YOU TO, YOU FUCKING BITCH!" he yells as his face turns red.

He is barely able to control his fury and tension.

"IS THAT THE ONLY REASON YOU ASKED ME TO MOVE IN WITH YOU?!?" she raises her voice loud enough for their neighbors to hear, who threaten to call the police for domestic abuse. "SO, YOU CAN USE ME FOR MY MONEY AND HAVE AN EXCUSE TO STOP GOING TO WORK?!?!"

"I'm not FUCKING talking about this anymore. I need to get out of here."

He grabs his phone, wallet, and keys, pushes past her, and storms out the front door.

"You need to cool your shit and calm the FUCK DOWN, or you'll fucking lose me forever!" he says to her as he slams the door, turns his car on, and drives away.

Still enraged, she punches a hole through the living room wall, furious that she had spent so much money on him while he had been lying to her this entire time.

Six hours and three holes in the wall later, she calms down, but he still does not come home.

'Where the hell is he?' she thinks to herself. 'Why isn't he coming home?'

She begins to worry that something had happened to him. She rapidly grabs her phone off the kitchen counter and calls him.

No answer.

She calls again, thinking that she had just dialed the wrong number.

Nothing.

She texts him, *Honey, are you okay? I'm so sorry about our fight. I love you so much. I don't mind paying the entire rent. I just want to be with you. Please come home.*

No reply.

An hour passes.

Still no reply.

She texts him again, *HONEY, PLEASE ANSWER ME. I JUST NEED TO KNOW THAT YOU'RE OKAY!*

No reply.

An hour passes.

Still no reply.

She calls him again, hoping to reach his voicemail.

No answer.

Nothing.

She continues to call him throughout the night, crying into her phone while overdosing on vodka, never knowing that he had blocked her number.

Betrayed

Three months after their first big argument, she is still suspicious about his intentions. After that night, he had refused to talk about the situation, and she had kept her thoughts and words to herself while continuing to engage in actions she deems unfair. She does not want that night to repeat itself as the thought of him leaving again tears her apart.

However, since that night, their relationship has not been the same. He spends more and more time on his computer, conversing with others, and less and less time with her. He smiles when he talks to his "friends" online but scours whenever he speaks to her.

She notices that he has been non-stop messaging several women on the Internet. When she questions him who the women are, he tells her they are just his friends and coworkers, and she has nothing to worry about.

One night, while he is off at work, she sneaks onto his computer, pulls up his search history, and reads his latest conversations with the "friends" he has been communicating with. They are not his friends.

He has been pouring his feelings out, emotionally, to at least three different women and has been calling them names such as "darling" and "honey," names he is only supposed to call her. He has been disclosing their relationship to these women, getting them to pity him while calling her a "bitch."

She feels completely betrayed and heartbroken. She scrolls up and sees that he has been having these conversations with them for months! How dare he!

How dare he flirt with other women when he is in a serious relationship with her! She fought with her mother for him, and she uplifted her entire life just for him! She scrolls up a bit more on one of the conversations and sees a picture of a half-naked woman wearing a leopard print bikini with a fake spray-on tan.

Below the picture reads, "I can't wait to feel you inside of me again."

She runs into the bathroom and vomits. She cannot believe her eyes. She hovers over the toilet bowl, tears and snot dripping from her nose as she grasps onto the side of the toilet bowl, fingers and palms sweating and trembling. She feels so betrayed, so disgusted.

She cannot believe what she just saw. She falls onto the bathroom floor after 30-minutes of vomiting, cradles into a child's pose, and sobs. Tears and mucus drip onto her tangled locks as she feels her heart beating out of her chest. The man she trusts and loves is a cheater.

Hours later, he comes home from work. She hears his car pull up and wonders if he had really been at work.

He walks into her sitting on the sofa, tearing up pictures of the two of them together, pictures she had given him last year for Christmas, pictures that represented their special moments together forever as a couple.

"What are you doing, honey?" he asks, confused and lethargic.

With dried-up tears on her cheeks, and her eyes gazing toward the floor, she quietly whispers, barely loud enough for him to hear, "I know."

"What? What do you know?" he responds, still puzzled.

"I know what you've been doing," she expresses in a shrill voice, this time loud enough for him to hear.

"What the fuck are you talking about, honey?" he questions her again while taking his coat off, flinging it onto the carpet, and snatching a soda from the fridge.

"Don't fucking call me 'honey'. I know you've been cheating on me!"

Her voice raises. Her anger begins to show as tears stream from her fatigued eyes.

He knows what she is referring to. However, he continues to play innocent so he can remain the victim.

"What the fuck are you talking about? I'm not cheating on you. I love you."

She points to his computer, and with tears continuing to stream down her face, she shouts, "I saw the messages on your computer. I know you've been flirting with other women online! I KNOW YOU'VE BEEN FUCKING SLEEPING WITH THEM!!"

"Why the FUCK were you on my computer?" he shrieks back at her, heatedly.

"That's not the point! You're cheating on me!" she retorts as she stands up from the sofa, throws the torn-up pictures onto the carpet, and spits on them.

"I told you not to FUCKING touch my computer! Stop spying on what I do! What I do with my own time, with my friends, is NONE OF YOUR BUSINESS!!"

He refuses to back down or confess his adultery. He can only fixate on how she betrayed him by touching his personal and private belongings.

"Who is she?" she asks as her tears now drip onto the carpet.

"Who is who?" he rolls his eyes, becoming bothered with her complaints and her accusations.

He pops open his soda, plops himself down onto his computer chair, and puts his headphones on.

She cannot stand when he tries to shut her out by putting his headphones on. She grabs her hair with both her hands and pulls with all her strength.

"The FUCKING HALF-NAKED girl you FUCKED!"

Fed up, he lobs his headphones off, stands up, and screeches, "None of your FUCKING BUSINESS!"

She becomes apprehensive and timid, fearful that he will storm out on her again.

"Do you still love me?"

Still irate, he mumbles quietly from under his breath.

"Of course, I do."

"Then stop flirting with THOSE WHORES!"

She proceeds to shed more tears, hoping her crying will make him feel sorry for her and apologize.

However, he does not notice and remains stubborn.

"I'm not flirting with them, and I don't like that you're accusing me of cheating on you when I'm not!"

"YES, YOU ARE!" she cries back, still in tears.

"If you don't like it, then GET THE FUCK OUT OF MY APARTMENT!"

She can see his face turn red the more she pushes him on this subject. She can see his eyes water from his wrath.

However, she continues pushing. Each time she considers backing down from the argument and apologizing, he mentions statements that make her mind want to explode.

"Your apartment!? I've been paying the FUCKING RENT for the PAST TEN MONTHS to live in this SHITTY HELLHOLE! THIS IS MY FUCKING APARTMENT!!"

"I DON'T FUCKING CARE! MY NAME IS ON THE LEASE, NOT YOURS, SO GET THE FUCK OUT OF MY APARTMENT!!"

He proceeds to forcefully push her out the door, refusing to let her speak or stay a second longer. He gathers her belongings, heaves them messily into a soiled garbage bag, and chucks the bag and her pooch violently out the door, slamming it behind her without saying a single word.

Livid, baffled, and still betrayed, she is at a loss for words. The battery on her phone is dead. She is thousands of dollars in debt. She quivers without a jacket while sitting on the curb outside his apartment in the dark, cold night.

She cannot comprehend how one simple conversation escalated so quickly. One minute, she is watching a reality show and eating popcorn on the sofa, and the next, she is being thrown out into the cold.

She begins to question all the decisions she had made that led her up to this point, and how she had chosen the wrong choice at every turn. She should have listened to her mother when she told her not to move in with him. She should have listened to her instinct when she knew her mother was right.

She should have done her research on the apartment before handing over all her money. She should have kept her mouth shut and not confront him about the women.

She is frightened. She grew up in the city so she had wandered out into the dark alone before. But this is different. This neighborhood is menacing. She has no car, no phone to call anyone, no money for a taxi, and no idea how the bus system works.

After sulking on the curb and pitying herself for an hour, she attempts to knock on his door, hoping that he has calmed down and will let her back in. She always had a way of using her words to win his heart, so she knows that she will have no problem talking her way back in.

She knocks, mentally preparing her apology speech for when he opens the door. She pictures how they will spend the night together after they make up. She will give him a back massage while he chooses his favorite movie to watch, and they will make love and fall asleep in each other's arms, remembering how much they still love each other.

She anxiously rubs her fingers together, preparing herself for when she sees his face so she can kiss him. Her heart shatters when he does not open the door.

She assumes it is because he is busy doing something, or he just has headphones on and cannot hear her knock. She knocks again and rubs her fingers together, hoping he will answer this time.

No answer.

'What the fuck is going on? Why won't he open the door?' she thinks to herself.

She looks through the window on the left side of the door. She sees him slouching in his new computer chair, without headphones, snacking on a bag of potato chips and pleasuring himself while looking at the picture of the half-naked woman.

Her heart shatters again. It has only been an hour, and he has already forgotten about her. How could he replace her so quickly? How long has he been cheating on her? How could she have been so naïve about what was going on?

Looking over at her freezing canine, she knows she has to get out of this cold and figure out a way to get home to her parents. She has no phone and no money, and it is already way past midnight.

Desperate, she wanders into the residential area of the destitute town, hoping she can find someone to let her borrow a phone or point her in the direction of a bus stop. She holds her frigid dog close to her chest as she stumbles down the dark, shady alleys, alleys full of drunks passed out on the curbs and junkies shooting up by the dumpsters.

She feels petrified and out of place as she continues to tread cautiously down the dark streets. She eventually finds a woman, walking from her car to her home, who points her in the direction of the closest bus.

She thanks the woman and proceeds to make her way toward the bus stop, three miles south from where she currently is. The further she walks, the more panicked she becomes, and she eventually drops her belongings, which were slowing her down, and runs toward the bus stop with her trembling dog curled up in her arms.

Her ugly clothing and toiletries can all be replaced; her life cannot. As she runs, she glances behind her, intermittently, to make sure no one is coming after her.

She is tired and hungry, and the cold makes it difficult to carry on. However, she has to keep going if she ever wants to make it back alive.

Roughly 45-minutes later, she sees a sign hidden behind a barren tree, reads it to make sure she is on the right side of the street, and waits, hoping that she has not already missed the last bus.

A long hour later, a bus drives by. She lifts her right arm and maniacally waves it up and down as she is not going to let this bus bypass her. The bus driver stops, and she gets on.

"Sorry, no dogs allowed," he tells her as he points to the sign above his head.

She rapidly explains her situation without taking a breath, crying and pouring her soul to him about how she is lost and has no way of getting home. She discloses her entire story of what happened with her boyfriend and how she just wants to get home.

Pitying her, he drives her to the closest stop near her parents, about six miles across the bridge with no other buses running in that direction until the next morning, forcing her to walk six miles home in the bleak darkness.

She thanks the bus driver and prepares herself for the long conversation she will have with her mother when she gets home, toes bleeding, legs frozen, and skin cracking.

***

A month passes since that traumatic night where her boyfriend kicked her out of his apartment. She had found her own apartment in the city and had signed the lease for a studio in a high-rise luxury apartment building. She has not spoken to her boyfriend since that night, repaired her relationship with her mother, and is thrilled to finally live on her own.

She tells herself, and her family, that she is ready to start over, to start living a life of independence and happiness.

However, shortly after moving in, she begins to feel lonely. She had not thought about her boyfriend while she was living with her parents because her mother had distracted her from her self-destructive thoughts.

Her loneliness soon kicks in at her new home and causes her to reach out to her boyfriend, against her better judgment.

They never officially broke up, and she hopes that he has been thinking about her as well. She texts him, begging for forgiveness and pleading for him to talk to her, pouring out her love for him and refusing to stop until he answers.

At first, he is reluctant to speak to her, which should have been her sign to let go and move on, but she persists.

A few weeks later, she convinces him to forgive her, despite her having done nothing wrong, and they begin seeing and speaking to each other again, despite her entire family telling her to stay away from him. They both still love each other, and she knows that love is enough for them to get through any obstacle in their relationship.

***

A couple of months after she moves into her own apartment, his lease ends, and he decides to move in with her. Again, her instinct tells her this is a terrible decision given the situation last time. She does not want a repeat of the past, and she knows that she WILL HAVE TO pay the entire rent by herself this time since the lease is under her name.

However, he assures her that he will help her out as much as he can, and so she agrees, pumping herself up again for a new life with him and starting over with her "soulmate."

She insists to her family that she has been on good terms with her boyfriend for about a year since the traumatic fight, and he assures her their relationship will be different and better this time around. Oblivious to reality, she, once again, ignores her mother's warnings, and she lets him move in with her, naively expecting things to change.

Living together again was remarkable, for the first couple of months. He does not help her with the rent and barely contributes to the finances as he had promised before he moved in. But she lets it go. She does not want a repeat of their argument by preemptively opening her mouth. She does not want to risk having him run away again.

They are together now, and that is all that matters to her at this moment. There are no more signs of him flirting with other women, and she assures herself that their relationship is back to normal, that she has him all to herself again. Her suspicions subside, and she finds herself caressing and laughing with the man she fell in love with on their first date all over again.

However, as patterns like to repeat themselves, she soon finds out his dirty secret. While they were living apart, but were still technically together, he moved in the woman he had cheated on her with after he kicked her out.

They lived together for a couple of months, played house and acted like a married couple, all while she was trying to piece their relationship back together. She also finds out that he had gone to this woman's apartment the night of their first argument about the rent and had fucked her multiple times that night.

Once again, she feels betrayed. She confronts him about this, and he accuses her again of snooping through his things, shouting that they were not "together" when he moved her in, even though they had never officially broken up. He storms out, refusing to be in contact for a week.

"FUCK!" she screams to herself. "What the FUCK did I do this time!?! I finally get him back, and I chase him away AGAIN!?"

She picks up her phone and frantically texts him.

I'm so sorry for snooping around on your computer. You're right. We were technically not together so it's not cheating if you moved another woman in while we were apart. I'm so sorry for accusing you of anything, and I take it all back. Please come home. Please forgive me! I love you! Please talk to me! Please don't be dead. I love you so much! Please forgive me and come home.

She hits send and cries on her bed for days, refusing to eat or go to work. A few days later, he comes home in the middle of the night, high as a kite. He sits down on the bed next to her, and she hugs him close without saying a single word. She is just glad that he is back. She has learned to stop questioning his actions so she could avoid causing him to walk away again.

A month before her lease ends, their relationship was at a good point: no more cheating, no more accusations, no more suspicions, no more running away, and all their secrets were out in the open. She feels like their relationship is finally getting back on track.

They begin apartment hunting together, searching for their new home, with him fully expecting her to pay a greater fraction of the rent because she has a higher salary than him. Although she knows this is not fair, instead of starting another argument and triggering him to leave, she agrees.

However, even though she is paying the majority of the rent, she does not have a say in the apartment she wants to live in. She knows her budget, and she knows what she can and cannot afford, but he insists that they spend more on a luxury apartment because it is their home, and they could both cover the costs by taking on more hours at work.

She is already working an 80-hour workweek but agrees anyway because she believes that he will finally follow through on his share. She assumes that because his name is now also on the lease, he would hold himself responsible for paying his half to avoid eviction.

During the first few months into their new apartment, he was helpful. He paid his share of the rent (his 25% share), gave her any extra money he had to try to help her out with additional bills and groceries, helped her pay for a fraction of the furniture, and bought groceries from where he worked once a month.

For the first time in their relationship, she feels like she finally has a partner. She is glad she fought for this relationship because he is doing whatever he can to also make this work. He clearly loves her.

But then the arguments start up again. Stupid arguments, not even ones that involve finances or infidelity, like the previous fights they have had.

They begin arguing about the types of groceries they buy because they each want different food, and they cannot afford to have two grocery lists.

They begin arguing about their sleep schedules because they work opposing hours so rather than spending time together when she gets home, he plays video games all day when she is at work and sleeps all night when she comes back, all while disturbing her sleep as he shouts with his friends in the middle of the night.

They begin arguing about how he refuses to clean his cat's litter even when the odor begins to fill the apartment, and they argue about how he refuses to wash the dishes, always waiting until she comes home to take care of them.

They begin arguing about how she always makes too much noise in her own apartment when he tries to stream videos to impress his ten followers.

They begin arguing about every little insignificant issue, almost to the point where they are actively looking for ways to pick fights with each other. The more she tries to juggle her 80-hour workweeks, the long travels, two pets, and endless arguments with a 28-year-old baby, the more depressed she gets, leading her to pull strands of her hair out every morning and cut into her skin with a small knife every night to relieve the pressure and anxiety.

She cannot tell her boyfriend how she feels. She cannot tell him that she is depressed and suicidal. One word about her emotions, and he instantly shuts off from her. He does not care about how she feels.

He only cares about how she can support him. He does not care that she has bald patches on her head and is on the brink of fainting every time she comes home. All he cares about is himself, and all she is allowed to care about is him.

Abused

Soon, their arguments become so strong that physical violence instigates, first toward the apartment, and then toward each other. Out of resentment and irritation, they smash the doors and cabinets in their apartment whenever they are frustrated with each other from all the disagreements.

He takes the groceries out of the fridge and hurls them onto the ground as an act that he no longer needs her money. She throws chairs against the doors and walls whenever he insults her and refuses to acknowledge her presence.

They both begin feeling out of control and disrespected, screaming hateful words toward each other and completely forgetting the promises they made to each other before they moved in together, promises where they would love each other no matter what happens.

She begins to rip strands of her hair out again, creating more obvious bald patches, cuts deeper into her arms and overdoses on pain reliever medications because she cannot bear to be in her own skin anymore.

She hates herself for allowing her life to become like this. She hates him for making her fall in love with him and then turning into an asshole. She hates this relationship for not playing out the way she had always dreamt of.

She knows she has to get out, but she also wants to continue loving him because she has already expended so much energy into him. She had sworn to herself, and to her family, that this relationship is going to work out, and she refuses to go against her pride.

She is sure she can make this relationship work if she can just push aside her opinions and her emotions. She is certain she can save this relationship if she can just give into his demands.

Then one day, he commits an act that he can never take back: he punches her in the face and bruises her left eye, engaging in the physical abuse he promised he would never do, but also creating the gateway for him to continue.

After he had hit her, he tells himself, and her, that they have to break up, that he can no longer be in a relationship where he is capable of hurting his partner.

He knows the relationship can never be the same after he has laid a hand on her.

He is smart. She is foolish. Even with a bruised eye, she continues to beg him not to go and continues to beg for forgiveness. She reasons that she deserves to be hit and convinces him to stay, allowing him to continue hitting her whenever she "misbehaves."

She covers her bruises whenever she goes out, telling others they are due to clumsiness rather than physical abuse. She reasons with herself by telling herself that he only hits her because he loves her and wants to remind her of it.

Her perception of love has become so distorted that she now associates physical and mental abuse with love. She does not allow her logical child to escape, even when it is screaming in agony to be let out.

They eventually make up, or so she likes to believe, and he promises to never lay another finger on her again other than out of love, a promise both him and her fail to realize will not last.

One month later, he proposes, giving her a cheap $30 ring that he eventually returns so he could use the money for his car insurance. She accepts, hugs him, and they both profess their love to each other.

They are engaged, ring or not, and she is ecstatic and over the moon. She cannot wait to spend the rest of her life with him, proudly calling him her "fiancé."

Bankrupt

Despite the engagement and despite her believing that, because he proposed, he will begin treating her with more respect, their relationship soon begins to fall apart again. The arguments start up, and as they increase, so do the physical abuse and his habit of calling out sick from work.

He has stopped caring about their finances, bringing in less and less money per month, and forcing her to open two new credit cards, denting her credit score, so she could cover his half and avoid getting evicted.

However, not only is she forced to cover the rent and their shared bills by herself, but she is also forced to cover his bills, bills that do not concern her, such as his car payments and insurance, as he guilt-trips her, once again, into doing so to prove her love for him.

Again, he promises her that he will keep sending his paychecks her way until he can repay her what he owes. With his track record, she doubts he can go through with his promise, as usual, but she decides to give him the benefit of the doubt as she has no other choice.

She can let it go and maintain the peace in their relationship, or she can fight him every step of the way and cause him to walk out again. Either way, she will not get her money back any sooner.

She is struggling. Her weight drops more and more each day as she barely touches their groceries just so they can last longer without her having to buy more. She steals sandwiches from work and turns them into her meals. The only person who eats their groceries is him, and he still complains about how there is never enough food in the apartment.

She cannot turn to her parents. She is too proud to admit to her family that she has made a huge mistake, once again, after they had warned her over and over again that she is making the wrong choice by being with him, and even more so, by moving in with him. She lies to her family and pretends that she has her finances covered and that she is exultant.

But, deep down, she is covering up more and more scars with each passing day.

One night, her fiancé heads off to work, strolls back in an hour later, and drops a bomb on her.

Distraught and quiet, he whispers, "Hey, honey, I'm home."

Flabbergasted that he is home so early, she questions him, confused.

"Hey! What are you doing home? Did they let you out early?"

"Nope, they fired me. They said I took too many sick days, and they told me to go home as soon as I went in."

He seems composed and less affected than he should be as he tells her that he had just lost his job.

She plays in her head what she wishes she could say to him.

'I FUCKING TOLD YOU SO! Are you that much of an idiot where you think you can take three days a week off and STILL keep your job?! Are you trying to fucking hurt me?! How the fuck are you supposed to pay me back now WITH NO JOB!?! YOU FUCKING IDIOT!'

However, rather than revealing her honest thoughts and triggering another conflict, she pretends to be compassionate and sympathetic.

"It's okay, honey. I'm sure you'll find another job soon. I trust that you will keep looking until you find one. I trust you won't let me down! In the meantime, I can handle our finances."

She thinks to herself again, infuriated, 'As I have already been fucking doing, you fucking piece of shit.'

She tries to hold back her ire as much as she can. All she wants to do is kick him out of her apartment because he has now become her ungrateful child rather than her partner and roommate.

He smiles weakly at her.

"I promise. I'll start job hunting tomorrow. Right now, I just want to lounge, play games with my friends, and be fat. I'm exhausted."

She fakes a smile back, continuing to hold back her rage and thinking, 'Exhausted!? You've been sitting around in your fucking boxers for the past five days, and you've only been at work for five minutes today!'

She is using all her strength to prevent herself from blowing up at him. She hates him for everything he has done to her. She hates him for using her for her money and making deceitful promises he never follows through on. Her instincts tell her to leave him and kick him out onto the streets as he had done to her. But her infatuation refuses to let her quit.

Her fear of loneliness refuses to let her give up on him. She fears that if she does not make it work with him, she will never find love again. She fears that the moment she kicks him out, that will be the moment he never returns.

"Alright, honey. Enjoy the rest of your night," she whispers to him as she slowly walks toward the bedroom, hoping he will ask to spend time with her, or at least give her a gesture to show gratification for everything she is doing for him.

Nothing.

Not even a kiss.

Not even a "good night."

Nothing.

As he plops down onto his chair, kicks back, and begins chatting with his friends.

She stumbles into their bedroom, feebly climbs into bed, and checks the balances on her credit cards.

$40,000 in credit card debt.

"FUCK!!" she shrieks as she throws her phone against the wall, curls up, and trembles with anxiety, all while hearing her fiancé laugh on the other side of the door, without a care in the world.

****

Two weeks pass since the layoff, and he continues to sit in front of his computer playing video games, without looking or applying for a single job.

She lets it go, keeping her patience with him, and still believing he will get around to it soon.

A month goes by.

Still nothing.

She begins to lose her tolerance but continues to have faith that he has tried looking.

Five months go by.

Still nothing.

"Hey, honey?" she asks, submissively, one morning.

With his eyes and mind distracted, he robotically answers without turning his head.

"What the hell do you want?"

"Have you tried looking for jobs yet?" she replies nervously.

"Yeah," he answers as if on autopilot.

"And?" she questions back.

"Stupid jobs that I don't want," he states to her as he continues to click, mindlessly, on his mouse.

Hesitant and afraid, she queries, "Well, can you just take any job that pays, even if you don't want it, while you continue looking so you can help me with the bills?"

That triggers him. He stops clicking, turns around, and looks up at her.

"Something I…don't…want…? I'm trying to build a fucking career here!!"

She bursts out into uncontrollable laughter, initially unaware that she is doing so.

"A career?!? You worked a shitty job for the past eight years at a supermarket stocking cans! Your biggest task was to make sure all the labels faced the right way! You were never even a manager! What kind of fucking career are you trying to build!? What, are you going to climb your stack of cans all the way TO THE FUCKING TOP!?"

And with that, she has broken her only promise to him: to never insult his career because that is the one part of him that he has always been insecure of. She had promised him that his career will never be something that drives her away because she loves him despite it.

He becomes defensive before she has the chance to take back her laughter.

"You fucking BITCH!! How dare you talk about my career like that!? I fucking hate it when you rub your career in my face, acting like a big shot just because you went to college. Who the fuck cares? At least I have morals!"

She laughs again, this time intentionally.

"Morals!?! What kind of messed up morals do you have when you, one, force me to rent an expensive apartment and leave me to PAY FOR IT BY MYSELF, and two, guilt-trip me into lending you money and LOSING YOUR JOB so you CAN'T EVEN PAY ME BACK!?!! A person with morals would at least settle for a shitty job to help out his FUCKING PARTNER!!"

He marches toward her, grabs her by her neck, rough enough to leave behind marks from his fingers.

"PARTNER?!! All you care about is money! You don't treat me like a partner! You treat me like a bank account. That's all you want from me. Well, you know what?! Even if I do get a job, you're not getting a single dime! FUCK YOU!"

He lets go, drops her onto the ground as she catches her breath, saunters back to his computer, puts on his headphones, and shuts her out, refusing to speak another word to her, leaving her to further question why she is still with him.

Chanced

Day after day, the arguments worsen. Night after night, she dreams about escaping him. She envisions how her life could be like with someone else, someone who does not beat her or force her into bankruptcy, someone whom she does not have to support.

Conversely, she also dreams about how much time and energy she has invested into this relationship, how many lies she has told others and herself that this relationship is perfect, and how much she has had to deal with to get him to stay with her.

Despite her opposing dreams, every morning as she wakes up before the sun rises, she pushes those thoughts aside, watches her fiancé drool over his keyboard in front of his desktop, takes her dog out, and hops on the bus for work.

After months of silence and resentment toward each other, her fiancé comes up to her one morning, still unemployed and speaking in full sentences for the first time in months, and tells her that he is moving in with his mother in another state.

He conveys that he still loves her, but he needs to go. He articulates that he can no longer be in an environment where he can lay a hand on her nor should she allow a situation like that to happen.

He tells her that he can no longer be in an environment where he feels disrespected. He voices that he can no longer be in a setting where he cannot eat what he wants like a grown man, and where he cannot engage in activities that he likes, such as play video games, without being chastised.

He expresses that, although she may be satisfied with it, he cannot live in an apartment where there are arguments 24/7.

She becomes furious. After years of remaining silent and giving him everything he wants, he STILL sees her as a selfish enemy.

"Are you seriously fucking blaming me for all this?! You're not innocent either! You hit me, you cheat on me, you put me in a shit ton of debt, and yet, I'm the bad guy here?!!"

"However you want to twist it, I'm leaving anyway, so I'll be out of your hair soon. Now you can't blame me for your negligent money problems. I won't need any of it anymore," he verbalizes while mocking her with his hands.

"No shit!! You already owe me thousands of dollars for your SHITTY CAR that you promised to pay me back for!" she screeches as she throws a vase to the ground and smashes it.

He continues to ignore her and blow her off, refusing to give into her manipulations.

"When I get a job back home, I will send you your money. Stop getting so uptight about money. This is why I'm leaving. You don't care about me; you just care about money."

Tears begin to flow from her eyes as she smashes another vase.

"I don't care about you?? Do you even realize the situation you're putting me in?! You CHOSE this apartment, PROMISING me that we will SHARE the rent. Now you're BAILING on me and making me pay for an apartment I CAN'T AFFORD?!"

"You've been paying the rent on your own for the past nine months. Clearly, you can afford it, and you're just trying to squeeze money out of me. Besides, just open more fucking credit cards to cover it. You don't fucking need my help, and I don't fucking NEED YOUR HELP!!" he laughs as he storms into the bedroom and slams the door behind him, popping off a screw.

She can hear him rustling through the door as he packs the rest of his clothes and shoes. She looks over at their mini Christmas tree. Their faux pine mini Christmas tree with two customized ornaments they had bought together the day he proposed to her.

She walks over to the tree, picks up the pink and white penguin her fiancé had chosen out for himself because he thought it represented him: silly, dorky, and lopsided. She chuckles to herself as she remembers the day he picked it up while shopping and started dancing up and down the aisles with it.

With this flashback, she remembers how much she still loves him, how much he had stolen her heart the first day she met him, how much they had promised to love each other despite all problems and obstacles, and how much they had planned their future together, husband and wife, hand in hand.

She knocks on the bedroom door.

"Go away!" he screams from the other side.

She opens the door anyway and walks in on him playing on his phone while lying in bed. She looks off to the side and sees his broken dresser overflowing with unkempt and questionably clean clothes while wrinkled garbage bags lay flat on the dusty carpet.

"Hey," she sighs quietly as she walks in and sits on the opposite side of the bed.

"I said, go away!" he replies, sternly, without looking up from his phone.

"Can we talk?" she asks, choking on her words.

"No" he responds stubbornly.

"Please?" she asks again.

She can sense his impatience rising.

With his eyes still gazed at his phone, he replies, "What do you want, bitch?"

She falls onto her knees and begins to plead with him.

"Please don't go. I love you. I'm sure we can make this work. I promise. Please just stay, and we can talk about it."

"There's nothing you can say that will make me stay. I'm leaving, and that's that."

He knows her tricks. He has been through this before. She always begs, yet, never changes. More importantly, he knows that the more he resists, the more she craves for him.

"Please just take a couple of days to think about it. We can talk through our problems, and I'm sure we can come up with a solution!" she continues to plead as she attempts to compromise while grabbing onto his arms.

"Fuck off! You had your chance, and you fucked it up. AGAIN! I'm tired of these fights. I have to go!"

He pushes her off him and kicks her to the ground.

Despite the internal and external pain, she refuses to stop. She still believes that the more she begs, the more likely he will break.

"Please! I'll skip work, and we can talk about it! You can even take your time finding a job that you want! I won't pressure you into anything! I promise! I know it's important for you to find something you want to turn into a career, and I fully support you! I'll take care of the finances until you can find something that fits!"

She can feel her stomach coming up through her throat and vomit forming as she speaks. She does not mean a single word of what she is saying. She is simply spilling out whatever she can to convince him to stay. Part of her is still unsure as to why.

"No! And stop pestering me to stay. My mind is made up! I'm leaving! Anything you say or do will just make it worse! All you are is a fucking liar! Just go to work, and I'll be out of your hair when you get home!" he retorts.

She becomes quiet and frightened as she sees flames forming in his eyes.

"Please don't go," she whispers again.

"GET OUT!!" he grabs her by her right ankle and drags her out of the bedroom, knocking her head against the door in the process.

Silenced and damaged, she stands up, hearing her bones crack as she does so, and goes off to work, unable to concentrate on anything, and still hoping that he will change his mind if she continues to text him all morning.

Maybe he will come to his senses while she is gone and stay after all. Maybe he will still be home when she gets back. Maybe he will get distracted while packing and will still be around so she can try to convince him to stay.

***

She rushes home from work after only four hours of non-stop wondering and finds her biggest fear: he is truly gone. His side of the bedroom is empty. His computer is gone. Everything he owns is gone. She knows he is not only gone temporarily because the last few times he stormed out and returned, he did not bring his computer with him.

She collapses onto the floor. Devastated. She rolls into a fetal position and bawls her eyes out while her pooch licks her tears and tramples over her head. She remains paralyzed for the next three hours, crying and sniffling until the only tears she has remaining are the tears pouring from inside her heart.

Obsessed

Over the next few weeks, she continues to feel emotionless as she locks herself in the apartment and refuses to see or speak to anyone. She has called out sick from work so many times that she has been put on probation.

She has not paid her bills, causing her credit score to drop dramatically. She has not eaten since the day he left, and she begins to waste away. She has not returned her mother's calls, causing her parents to knock on the apartment door, each time met with no answer.

She cannot remember a time where she has felt so broken and so depressed. She reminisces back to all the times when she has felt low and depressed, and he was always there to lift her spirits. She remembers how, during their positive moments, she had never felt happier and more optimistic about her life.

She wants him back. She needs him back. He is the only person who can pull her out of this cloud of misery. He is the only person who can make her fall in love with life again. He is the only person she wants in her life.

She refuses to quit on their relationship, despite the pain she had dealt with while she was in it, the relationship that only seems to exist in her mind. She is positive that he still loves her, and that he still wants to be with her. She is willing to do whatever it takes to get him to realize that they are meant to be together and come home.

She spends hours constructing emails, pouring her heart out, expressing how much she loves him and typing out every possible heartbroken cliché she can think of to get him to feel sorry for her, realize how much she is hurting, and speak to her again.

Ever since you left, my world has fallen apart. I cannot eat. I cannot move. I cannot focus. All I can think about is you and how much I am hurting without you. All I want in life is you.

I don't care about money. I don't care if you spend time with me or not. I don't care if you spend the rest of your life playing video games with your friends while I support you. I don't care if you never pay me back. I don't even mind supporting you the rest of my life.

Please come back to me, honey. Please come home. I don't want to live in this world without you. I never want to love anyone else besides you. I will move to you if you don't want to move back. I will go anywhere you want to go. I don't care about anything except being able to spend the rest of my life with you.

I want that life that we planned together, that happy family and that happy life that we always talked about. I don't care about a ring. I don't care about a fancy wedding. I don't care that you hit me and that you cheated on me. I deserved all of it. I care about you. I know you only hurt me because you were hurt. I'm sorry. I love you so much.

If you come home, I promise to give you everything you want. I promise to be there for you through thick and thin. I promise to never start another argument even if I want to, and I promise to love you forever.

Please come home. Please come home to me. I do not want to live if I cannot live with you.

I love you.

Please come back.

However, rather than receiving the response she optimistically expects, she receives one single email telling her to go fuck herself, and he proceeds to block her from all forms of communication, phone and social media included. The only access she has left to him is through email, which he refuses to respond to. She panics.

She freaks. She starts ripping her hair out again as she is unable to deal with the apprehension that comes with not having control of this situation.

She frantically logs into her social media account and hits up his family, friends, and coworkers, sending them pity emails and trying to get them to convince him to talk to her. Eighteen messages and emails later, zero responses and twelve blocks. She then begins to stalk their profiles, trying to see if they posted pictures of her fiancé so she can at least keep tabs on his life.

Nothing.

Three weeks later, she receives an email from him. She is thrilled, and she is sure that this is an email from him telling her that he misses her and wants to get back together. Fingers crossed and hopes up, she frantically opens her email. Her heart stops. It is not the email she had hoped for.

Instead, it is an email from him telling her to leave his family and friends alone. He tells her that she is a crazy and psychotic bitch who cannot get the hint that he is no longer interested in her and that he has moved onto someone else.

Nevertheless, that does not stop her. She was able to catch his attention, despite the method she used to do so, and she craves for more. She sinks into more drastic measures, stalking and contacting all the women he has ever dated and has ever cheated on her with, asking them to spill information about him, and even asking them to apologize to him for her.

Again, she was met with silence.

Nothing.

No response.

No one acknowledges her, and no one cares that she is suffering.

The loss of attention drives her insane.

She needs to be loved.

She lives on affection.

She will not stop until she fulfills her wishes and her desires.

She constructs ten fake social media aliases, with full profiles for each one, as a way of luring him in by pretending to be interested in him. She fashions sham dating profiles of gorgeous and joyful women so she can attempt to get him to speak to her through the fake profiles. However, despite her best efforts, he remains radio silent.

No answer.

No response.

Nothing.

She continues to lock herself in the apartment, sitting in a dark corner of the bedroom cutting her arm, and obsessively emails everyone until someone responds.

She looks in her mirror, and she no longer recognizes herself. Her hair is tangled and frayed. Her cheeks are jaunt from the lack of nourishment. Her eyes are sunken with bags due to the lack of sleep.

She takes the small pocket knife she has been using to cut her arm and makes a deep cut from her bottom lip down to her chin.

She does not feel pain. She is still traumatized by her heartbreak. She no longer knows who she is as she writes "Bitch" with deep, red lipstick on the off-white walls in the dark, candlelit bedroom.

Repeated

Four months pass, and he eventually unblocks her and sends her a text. She hears her phone go off, drops her knife, and eagerly unlocks her phone. His text says he still loves her, and she becomes overwhelmed with excitement and bliss. She knew he would come around, and she responds with how much she loves him and how much she misses him.

She no longer feels emotionless, and she spends her days messaging him, anxiously waiting by her phone for his responses, disregarding all her responsibilities, night after night.

They continue messaging back and forth, first with small talk and catching up on what has happened since they have been apart. She lies and says she has been focused on work and her online business while finding out that he has been serial dating.

But she lets it go. She tries to ignore all the women he has dated. She tries to forget how many women he has been with since he left. She has him back now, and she promises herself that she will never let him go again. She tells herself that he had the chance to move on and date others, and because he STILL came back to her, then he must truly love her.

Eventually, they begin engaging in deeper conversations, conversations about how much they both still love each other and how much they still want to be in each other's lives. They chat about how happy they were at the beginning of their relationship and how it spiraled downhill so quickly.

He tells her that he is thinking of moving back in with her and giving their relationship another chance. She is euphoric. She knew he would change his mind and come back if she just waits for him long enough. She promises him that their lives will be different this time around, and that she will no longer pester him to help out with finances or to spend time with her.

She promises him that she will give him all the space he wants to be alone and to stream his video games, and that she will wait for him to come to her, only on his own terms and if he chooses to.

They are both immature and oblivious. None of their problems have been addressed, and they both know that she will not follow through on her promises.

He moves back in after almost a year of being away, and they fall head-over-heels for each other once again, loving and cherishing each other every night. He watches movies with her that he does not like. She listens to him explain his video games and streaming even though she finds them extremely dull.

He gets a new job and goes into work consistently, helping her out with finances whenever he can even though she had promised him that he would not have to. She sees him as a true partner again, a partner who loves and cares about her, a partner who will be there for her no matter what, the partner she had always wanted.

However, because their issues were never addressed, the arguments soon begin to creep up. The problems that were there before he left were all still there when he came back. After a few short weeks, she becomes bothered with how much time he spends with his friends and his games rather than with her, and she continues to pressure him to give back the money he owes her whenever she feels like she is struggling financially.

Despite their problems and their issues, they continue moving forward, still believing that they are meant to be with each other and that they can overcome any obstacle. Their lease is finally coming to an end, and they begin looking for another apartment.

Given what had happened, she knows that she has to find a cheaper apartment to avoid accumulating more debt. However, she gives into his demands, once again, when he suggests that they move into an apartment even more expensive than the one they currently have.

She tries to talk him out of it and into finding something half the cost as she reminds him of their financial status. He assures her that his new job is paying him more than he used to make, and he promises to go into work every day now that they have stopped arguing every night.

Hesitant and concerned, she signs the lease anyway, foolishly believing that he will come through. He helps her pay for the security deposit, which further assures her that he is going to follow through this time.

After a few short weeks into their new apartment, she encounters more financial disturbances. He calls her from work one night and tells her that his car has been towed because he had failed to make payments on time.

He pressures her into handing over $300 for the tow and an additional $8,000 for the late car payments, coercing her to request credit increases on both her credit cards, further putting a dent in her credit score.

The cycle continues. She hands over her money. He feels his burdens lifted from his shoulders and stops going into work because of the lack of responsibility. The more times he calls out, the more frustrated she begins to get.

"You're calling out again? You haven't gone into work all week. What's going on?" she asks as she tries to hold back her anger.

Unsurprisingly, he simply shrugs her off, brushing their problems off his shoulder like they are not important.

"Nothing. I just don't feel like going in."

Baffled and still trying to hold back, "But it's your job. You have to go in, or you're going to get fired again."

"Stop being paranoid. I'm not going to get fired," he responds sternly.

"Can you please just go in? We need the money," she continues to solicit him as her voice begins to scratch.

"HEY!" he barks. "You promised you weren't going to pressure me for money anymore. You'll get your money back when you get your money back. Now please leave me alone. I'M HANGING WITH MY FRIENDS!"

He puts his headphones back on, she punches another hole through the wall, and she becomes more suicidal. She feels unable to escape from the debt she has dug herself into. She feels like her cycle of misfortune will never come to an end. The more she reflects on how her life will never change, the more she proceeds to pull her hair out and cut herself. She has been wearing a wig ever since he moved back in.

Not once did he notice.

No one ever notices how she struggles.

She always hides her pain with smiles and laughter.

No one ever notices the damage behind her walls.

Even if they do, will they even care?

The quarrels intensify. The physical fights commence.

More and more chairs are being thrown against the walls and toward each other, and she just wants it all to stop. She has blown over $40,000 on him, personal payments and rent included, and he still does not give a fuck about her.

She realizes that they are having difficulties, but she is still so sure that they can work through anything this time around that she fails to give the struggles much thought. They dispute. They heave furniture at each other. They fall asleep. They reconcile the next morning.

However, one day, she comes home from work and finds herself standing alone in an empty apartment with nothing around except for her dog and her clothes.

She looks around the living room and into the kitchen. All their furniture, television, sofa, lamps, tables, his computer and desk included, their groceries, and their appliances, are all missing. She looks inside the bedroom and sees the bed, the dressers, and his side of the room gone, all except for her corner of self-regret.

She panics.

She reaches for her phone and calls her fiancé.

No answer.

She tries calling again. As the phone rings, she sees a small note taped onto the kitchen wall.

I can't live like this anymore. I'm sick and tired of all the arguing and fighting. It makes me sick to my stomach that we can't just get along. We need to break up for good.

I'm done with this relationship. I sold all our furniture to make some extra money, and I took everything else with me to move in with a girl I've been flirting with while we've been fighting. I know you want out of this relationship just as much as I do.

I'm also not going to pay you back because I need this money more than you do. I don't ever want to talk to you again. Please don't text me. Please don't contact me. Goodbye.

With that, she drops the note onto the tiled kitchen floor and freezes, all alone in an empty apartment, all alone in the world.

Fallen

She wakes up, gasping from her flashback. She springs up from the blood-stained ground and chokes on her saliva. She rubs her fingerless hands together.

The blood has stopped dripping.

Her bones still exposed.

Her hands have become numb from the lack of sensation.

Her surrounding is still dark.

She is still trapped inside the fucking box.

She cannot remember the events that led her from her empty apartment into a dark, cold metal box.

What the hell happened? Did he come back, whack her against the back of her head, and lock her inside a box?

What the fuck is she doing in a box? Did someone else come in after he had left and kidnap her? Did she forget to lock the fucking door?

"FUCK!!!" she bellows.

She holds her knees tightly to her chest and rocks back and forth.

Back and forth.

Back and forth.

Back and forth.

"I can't do this anymore. I can't do this anymore," she chants repeatedly.

"I HAVE TO FUCKING GET OUT OF THIS SHITHOLE!!" she shrieks out loud as she pounds her fists against the walls again.

However, no one answers her.

No one cares.

She loses hope.

She just wants this to be over with.

She closes her eyes, mentally prepares herself, and with one quick and aggressive blow, she smashes her head against the metal wall in front of her.

Silence.

Breathless.
Gone.

Revealed

While her relationship was detrimental, with a man who lured her in only to use and leave her in the end, her greatest enemy was ultimately herself.

She had so many chances to leave, so many opportunities to see all the reasons they should not have been together and walk away. Her fiancé had shown her many red flags that she refused to accept. She should have walked away at the first sign of infidelity.

She should have run as far as she could when he first laid his hand on her. She should have shut him out of her life the first time he had moved out instead of doing everything she did to bring him back.

However, she refused to acknowledge the truth. She remained stuck inside her own head. She wanted the relationship to work out so badly that she pushed aside her logic and common sense and instead, followed her impulsive and desperate instinct to hunt down one goal: to get him back.

She created a version of herself that was hungry for constant love, even though the love she received was abusive. She created a version of herself where she felt paralyzed to everything else except him. She created a version of herself that she ultimately despised.

Her external relationship with her fiancé may have damaged her physically and mentally, but her internal relationship with herself had destroyed her. The box she was trapped inside of is her true persona trapped inside her own mind, pleading to be released.

Her mind had become so distorted that she was no longer able to distinguish abuse from love. She had pushed her knowledge aside for so long that she no longer knew what it meant to have a conscience.

She had so many chances.

So many chances to find someone new.

So many chances to run toward a life of happiness.

So many chances to walk away from a life that was killing her.

So many chances to prevent her sufferings and her eventual death.

Why did she stay?

Why did she stay in a relationship where she was neglected?

Why did she stay in a relationship with an unfaithful man?

Why did she stay in a relationship with someone who abused her?

Why did she hold onto a partner who just wanted out?

Why did she hold onto a man she no longer loved?

Because she was afraid.

Afraid to admit to herself that she had messed up.

Afraid to admit to herself that she had failed.

Afraid to admit to herself that she had made wrong choices at every obvious turn.

Afraid to admit to herself that she had found love and lost it.

Afraid to admit to herself that she had allowed someone to abuse her time after time.

Afraid to admit to herself that her life will be lonely if she lets go.

Afraid to admit to herself that she has flaws.

The Human Psyche

Sigmund Freud delineated the human psyche as three distinct levels of the mind: the preconscious mind, the subconscious mind, and the unconscious mind.

The preconscious mind manifests in our preemptive thoughts that have been untouched by logic and awareness. The conscious mind manifests in our awareness, our thoughts, and our emotions, a state of mental processing and rationality that stabilizes the urges of the Id. The unconscious mind manifests outside our conscious awareness, portraying as emotions we are not aware of such as anxiety or depression.

The three levels of the mind can be applied to love. Our cravings and desires come into awareness when we encounter new partners, and we become unaware of the dark sides of new relationships because we remain in the conscious phase of being in love.

We fail to acknowledge when our relationships go awry because we become unaware of the instabilities and negativity that happen until it is too late.

Staying in an abusive relationship can be compared to drug addiction. We experience positive or negative reinforcements, such as being "punished" for speaking the wrong words and behaving in ways unexpected or being "rewarded" for obeying the "rules" and behaving in ways we are told.

When we are "rewarded," our bodies experience spiked levels of dopamine that continue to make us crave for more "rewards" from our abusers. This system of give and take ultimately results in those abused becoming desperate and blaming themselves while trying to win the love of those who take advantage of them.

Abusive relationships all tend to follow the same pattern, where those maltreated are enticed by the charm of their abusers to the point where they begin to idolize and worship them. They are then disrespected and devalued, and ultimately discarded and destroyed, leaving the mind confused and desperate to hold on by any means possible without fully understanding why.

Common fears that prevent victims from leaving their abusers, resulting in endless intrapsychic battles, include the fear of what could potentially happen to them if they leave, the belief that fighting for relationships equates to strength and love, the shame that comes with admitting failure when a long-term relationship ends in divorce, the low self-esteem that comes from the constant mental and emotional abuse toward the self, and the blinded love and infatuation that comes with holding onto an image of the abuser that no longer exists.

Sadistic relationships often correlate with obsessive affection, with the obsession stemming from lack of closure, or rather lack of closure with ourselves. Even when our partners lay out the specific reasons why they longer want to be with us, we refuse to accept the truth, and instead, hold out for the answers that align with what we want, pressuring and convincing our partners to give us second chances.

The quote, "We want what we cannot have" continues to hold true when we pursue those who no longer want us.

When abusers walk away rather than vice versa, our minds automatically point toward self-blame and guilt.

We blindly see their departures as signs that we have done something wrong and that we need to take action to repair the relationships.

We are left with constant thoughts and doubts about the flaws we possess that have forced our partners to walk out.

We are left with extreme self-hate and negativity that plague our minds to believe that we deserve to be abused.

We are left with resentment toward ourselves for not having been strong enough to persist in a life-threatening relationship.

We are left confused and entrapped in a mind-warp where we continue to justify our pain.

We are left with the deceit of no longer knowing who we are.

Broken &

Abused

The Imprisoned Mind

Broken & Abused
The Imprisoned Mind